Disappearance

Wanda Choirs

Copyright © 2023 by Wanda Choirs

All rights reserved.

No portion of this book may be reproduced in any form without written permission from the publisher or author, except as permitted by U.S. copyright law.

Contents

Chapter 1	1
Chapter 2	5
Chapter 3	9
Chapter 4	13
Chapter 5	17
Chapter 6	23
Chapter 7	27
Chapter 8	31
Chapter 9	36
Chapter 10	41
Chapter 11	45
Chapter 12	49
Chapter 13	54
Chapter 14	58
Chapter 15	62

Chapter 16	66
Chapter 17	70
Chapter 18	74
The End	78

Contents

Chapter 1	1
Chapter 2	5
Chapter 3	9
Chapter 4	13
Chapter 5	17
Chapter 6	23
Chapter 7	27
Chapter 8	31
Chapter 9	36
Chapter 10	41
Chapter 11	45
Chapter 12	49
Chapter 13	54
Chapter 14	58
Chapter 15	62

Chapter 16	66
Chapter 17	70
Chapter 18	74
The End	78

Chapter 1

● MARLOWE•

Making my bed I hear keys at the door causing me to look over as it opens and Ike walks in.

"You ready for your session today". He asked as we walked out of my room.

"Yeah I only have about a few more before I'm done". I said smiling as we walked out of the ward.

"You came a long way these last few months of me watching you". He said opening the van door for me.

"Trying to get better for my daughter". I said as he helped me inside.

Closing the door he gets in the drivers side and starts the van up as I put my seat belt on.

"Are you excited about getting released". He asked looking at me through the rear view mirror.

"Yeah a fresh start is what I need". I said and he nodded.

The rest of the ride was quiet as music played on the radio.

|35 minutes later|

Getting out of the hospital van I thank the man that watches my ward before closing the door and walking into the building.

"Hello who are you here to see". The receptionist asked.

"I have a 3 o'clock with Leanna". I said looking around the foyer.

"Sure take a seat right outside her office". She said pointing over to the seats.

"Thank you". I said giving her a small smile before walking away and taking a seat.

Sitting outside the office I wait for the therapist to call me back as I rub my stomach. I didn't think I would be where I was today but here I am.

The door to the office opened up and I see a girl walk out with my therapist Leanna behind her. They talked for a little bit before she looked over and gestured for me to come to her.

Standing up I make my way inside of the office taking a seat on the couch.

"So how have you been". She asked taking a seat in the chair In front of me.

"I've been doing good I found an cheap apartment to stay in, the hospital is releasing me Friday".I said with a small smile on my face.

"Have you had any urges". She asked writing in her notepad.

"Not for a few months it's an on and off again type of thing". I said rubbing my hands up and down my legs and she watched me before writing.

"And the babies father where is he". She asked causing me to sigh.

"He's somewhere around here doing something ". I said twisting my mouth to the side with a shrug.

"What do you think you can offer the baby you have no income, no clothing, food, or furniture for the baby do you ever think about giving her up". She said causing me to scrunch up my face.

"I can offer her love". I said and she laughed a little.

"That's not enough". She said shaking her head before she started writing on that notepad again.

"Can I ask you something". I ask causing her to look up at me.

"Sure go ahead". She said putting her pen down.

"How do I get to that point where I can be better for my daughter I mean the hospital still has me on watch thinking I will harm her". I said rolling my eyes.

"That's a question you would have to ask yourself". She said staring at me.

"I can't really do anything about my emotions it's a medical disorder but I guess the only thing I can do is try to stay in a happy mood so I don't get those urges". I said and she nodded.

"I'm going to give you some homework". She said sitting up.

"I want you to go home and think about things that make you happy and then put them into action". She said writing something on a piece of paper and handing it to me.

The timer went off letting me know our time was up. Standing up I make my way out of the office and the people were already waiting to take me back to the hospital.

"How was it". Ike asked helping me into the van.

"It was okay". I said shrugging my shoulders and he nods before closing the door and getting in the drivers seat.

Laying my head back I close my eyes...

Chapter 2

Friday| •MARLOWE•

I woke up around 5 this morning to pack the rest of my things. I had a good amount of things from staying here for a few months.

As I was zipping you one of my suitcases the locks on the door could be heard turning before it opened.

"I knew you were up early you want to come down and eat". Ike asked standing in the doorway.

"Yeah I could eat". I said following him out of the room.

"Marlowe how does it feel to be leaving". Brent asked following us to the dinning area.

"It feels great to know I won't be watched 24/7". I said as we both laughed.

Brent is a 46 year old man that has be here for years who knows when or if they'll let him out. He has these episodes that they deem unsafe. And as for Ike he's like the father I never had.

"You know Pamela is coming to visit me today". He said talking about his deceased wife.

"Brent your wife is dead". One of the workers said as we grabbed our plates and took a seat at a table.

"DON'T YOU...don't you say that".He said slamming his hands on the table causing everyone to look over at us.

"Hey hey it's okay he doesn't know what he's talking about Pamela will be here". I said grabbing his hand giving it a squeeze and he calmed down taking a seat.

"Yeah she'll be here". He mumbled to himself picking up his fork.

"Reese why do you do this every time". Ike asked with a frown on his face.

"What it's fun to see the old man go psycho". He said laughing as he folded his arms.

Shaking my head I just start to eat and make small conversation with Brent.

|15 minutes later|

After finishing my food I make my way back to my room. Taking the suitcase off of my bed I roll it to the door along with the other one before taking a seat on the bed.

"Knock knock your cabs here". Ike said knocking on the door.

Standing up I make my way over to the door and go to grab the suitcases when he shakes his head grabbing them.

"Just get the bag". He said and I nodded picking it up before following him to the front.

Stopping at the desk I sign my name to be released and walk out to the cab that was parked out front. The driver gets out and takes my bag from me helping Ike out my things in the trunk as I got in the car.

"You be safe". Ike said leaning down into the window.

"I will". I said and he talked the top of the hood and the driver pulled off.

|1 hour later|

I get excited seeing us pull up in front of my new apartment. Getting out of the car he gets my things and closes the trunk.

"I'll carry them just lead the way". He said and I nodded making my way inside the building.

Looking at all the numbers I stop In front of my apartment door and unlock it. The driver sits my things down and I hand him the money Ike gave me to pay him with.

"Thank you have a great day". He said walking away.

I pick up the bag and roll the two suitcases inside before closing the door and looking around.

I had a donated dining and living room set. As for my room Ike made sure it was a new bedroom set. Ike got me what he could for my apartment and I really appreciate him for that.

I make my way to the back and start putting my things away.

|45 minutes later|

I walk out of my room and to the other room that was empty and bare. I wanted to decorate the room myself and I would have to get to it soon with my Babygirl coming.

Looking around the room one more time I walk out and back to my room taking my shoes off before lying down on the bed.

It feels good to be out of that place...

PLEASE EXCUSE ANY MISTAKES #COMMENT#VOTE

Chapter 3

(A/N: Jahreem is pronounced Dream in this book)

•MARLOWE•

With the baby coming soon I thought I should get in contact with her father to see what he's wants to do after she's born. He usually hangs in front of the grocery market with his little friends so I'm hoping to run into him today.

Since I already took a shower I just slid my flip flops on and grabbed my keys walking out the front door. Locking it I make my way out of the apartment and down the street.

Walking up the street from the grocery market I see Jahreem exactly where I expected him to be.

"Jahreem can I talk to you". I ask walking up and standing in front of him.

"Wassup". He asked looking down at me.

"I finally got a place and I'm doing better". I said smiling up at him.

"That's good have you thought about what we talked about". He asked and I nodded my head.

"I decided I was going to keep the baby". I said fiddling with my fingers.

"I'm not ready for no kid right now but good luck with that". He said causing his friends to laugh and slap hands with him.

"You think that's cute showing out for bum niggas that don't got a job standing on corners and shit". I ask with my face scrunched up and they all stop laughing.

"Yo bitch you don't know what the fuck you talking about". One of them said trying to walk up on me.

"See now hold the fuck up don't be walking up on her like that you know what I'm on". Jahreem said getting in the boys face.

"Y'all chill out". Another boy said stepping in between the two.

"Look let's go". Jahreem said grabbing my hand and leading me into the market.

"Why you coming up talking shit". He asked and I shrugged my shoulder.

"I know, you do that shit cause you know I'm not gone let nobody disrespect you". He said as we both laughed.

"I wasn't even talking to him he just always want to act like billy bad ass y'all ain't gone get nowhere trying to impress each other". I said placing some watermelon slices in the basket he picked up.

"Look about what I said back there I'm as ready as I can get and I been there for every appointment and shit so if that don't show you I want this I don't know what will". He said rubbing my stomach as I looked at what type of meat I wanted.

"I know you was just talking out the side of your neck but you need to stop that". I said picking the thin sliced turkey meat.

"I am but how long you been out". He asked as we walked up to the register.

"I got out yesterday". I said paying for my things.

"So the urges went away". He asked as we walked out of the store and down the street.

"For the most part but I still get that voice inside my head that tells me to end it all". I said and I could see him look over at me from my peripheral vision as I looked at the ground.

"They gave you some medicine to take". He asked and I shook my head.

"The medicine they wanted to prescribe me with could harm the baby so I'm controlling it the best way I can". I said as we walked into my apartment.

"This straight what the baby room looking like". He asked and I sat the bags on the counter before stowing him to the baby room.

"We need to get this done ASAP she almost here". He said and I nodded.

"Look I get paid this Thursday so we gone go ahead and decorate this room". He said as we walked out of the room.

"You got a tv in yo room". He asked and I nodded guiding him to the back.

Taking off our shoes we get in bed and cut the tv on.

"You think she gone think I'm a good father". He asked looking down at me as I laid on his chest.

"If you do right by her then of course she will". I said giving him a small smile.

"Oh trust she gone be annoyed with my ass like why this nigga always around". He said causing us both to laugh.

"She'll get used to it". I said and he shook his head.

"I'm gone be clingy as fuck". He said nodding his head with a smile as he rubbed my stomach.

"When you don't be trying to show out for yo niggas you really a sweetheart". I said and he smacked his lips.

"Just got to make them niggas think I don't give a fuck about nothing so they don't test me". He said and I nodded even though I don't completely agree with it.

"I mean people gone text you everyday but this subway so have it your way". I said with a shrug and he slaps my butt as we laughed.

"Shut up and watch the movie". He said as he got a little more comfortable.

"I can't wait till you get here". He whispered still rubbing my stomach.

We might not have much but she's going to be loved...

PLEASE EXCUSE ANY MISTAKES #COMMENT#VOTE

Chapter 4

|3 months later| •JAHREEM•

I woke up early this morning to get ready for work. I work at the warehouse from four in the morning till three in the afternoon. I do four 12 hour days and Marlowe thinks I be out running the streets when she wake up but I really be at work.

Grabbing my car keys off of the dresser I walk over to her side and lean down kissing her forehead before bending down farther and kissing her stomach.

"I love you babygirl". I whispered before standing up straight and walking out of the room.

Going into the kitchen I go In the fridge and get my lunch I packed last night. I grab an apple on my way out and lock the door walking to my car.

Getting in I start it up and drive off.

|20 minutes later|

Parking the car I cut it off and grab my lunch bag getting out of the car. Locking it I make my way inside the building and scan my badge walking through the door.

Putting my food in the fridge I go to my locker and grab my hard hat and put it on.

"How you doing this morning young buck". An Og that's been here for a while asked.

"I'm doing good". I said taking a seat on the bench.

"How's that baby room coming along". He asked looking over at me as he looked for something in his locker.

"So far me and my girl painted it and got a few clothes but with this lil check I can get a cheap lil crib and some decorations for my babygirl room I mean that's gone be kind of my whole check but that's why I'm here early mornings". I said lacing you my steel toe boots.

"That's good son". He said and I nod standing up.

"Yeah I got to get out there though I'll talk to you later". I said patting his shoulder on the way past him.

Walking into the actual warehouse part I could hear forklifts beeping and machines running.

"Let's get this shit over with". I mumbled to myself as I put my gloves on.

|3 o'clock|

Swiping my id I walk out of the building and get in car starting it up pulling off.

On my way to the house I stop by Walmart to go pick up the crib I ordered on my break.

With the help of an employee we get it in my backseat.

"Thanks man". I said slapping hands with the boy that helped me.

"No problem dude and congratulations". He said causing me to smile thinking about my daughter.

"Thank you". I said closing the door before making my way to the drivers side and getting in.

Starting the car up I pull off towards the apartments.

Once I finally make it I take it out of the backseat before making way way inside the apartment building.

Unlocking the door Marlowe was sitting on the couch watching tv until she heard me coming in.

"What is this wait where did you get the money for this". She asked standing up from the couch as I pushed it inside and closed the door.

"You like it". I ask and she nodded looking at it before looking at me.

"I'm about to go set it up". I said pushing it to the nursery.

"But where did the money come from". She asked following behind me.

"I got a job". I said looking over at her and she started smiling.

"What no way I'm so proud of you I thought you would never leave the streets". She said and I shook my head.

"I ain't fully out yet but this is a step towards it so we can live comfortably with our daughter and not have to worry about enemies". I said opening up the box with some scissors.

"So where do you work". She asked taking a seat in the rocking chair.

"Stanleys warehouse". I said and she nodded her head.

"It ain't much money I spent all of the money on this crib and I got 100 left over for a little groceries". I said and she sighed looking down like she was about to cry.

"What's wrong baby". I ask walking over and kneeling down in front of her.

"We can't give her nice things we barely have enough money to pay the bills and get groceries". She said wiping her face.

"Hey hey hey look at me as long as she knows she got two parents that love her she won't be worried about all that other shit". I said holding her face in my hands as I stared at her.

"You hear me". I ask and she nodded.

I lean up and kiss her before standing up.

"Let's set up babygirl crib". I said causing her to smile and she stood up walking towards the box.

We gone be straight I'll make sure of that...

PLEASE EXCUSE ANY MISTAKES #COMMENT#VOTE

Chapter 5

1 month later| •MARLOWE•

I've been having contractions all morning so Jahreem decided to take off work to stay with me.

"Baby you alright you want some soup". He asked and I nodded my head.

"Can you carry me to the living room". I ask and he nods his head before picking me up bridal style.

"Damn". He said and I hit his chest softly as we laughed.

"You weak as hell". I said causing us both to laugh.

"Stop playing with me". I said as he placed me on the couch.

"After you eat this soup I'm gone go get your shoes and the baby bag". He said grabbing the remote from by the tv and handing it to me.

"Okay". I said rubbing my stomach.

"I can't believe my baby girl about to be here". He said walking back to me with the soup.

"I know and she's ready to come out". I said as he sat on the couch and started rubbing my stomach.

|15 minutes later|

We were now in the car on our way to the hospital. The ride was silent and the only thing that could be heard is the music.

Jahreem reaches over rubbing my stomach as I laid back into my seat.

"I packed her this outfit it's gone make you jealous". He said causing me to look over at him.

"It better not have no stupid shit on it". I said causing him to laugh.

"It ain't stupid bro". He said smiling looking from me to the road.

"Just get me to the hospital". I said closing my eyes.

|Hospital|

Checking in they gave us a room and said the doctor would be in after he got done with a patient.

"I can't believe your water broke yesterday night like how is that shit possible". Jahreem said with a confused look on his face.

"Babe I'm in a lot of pain right now so can you please be quiet". I say holding his hand as he sat by the bed.

"Yeah my bad". He said before looking over at the tv.

|MEANWHILE|

"Doctor we have a baby that was just dropped off in critical condition". One of the nurses said making their way into my office.

"Alright I'll be on my way". I said covering the end of the phone.

He nodded before walking out.

"Why can't I just have one baby it's not fair". My wife said crying on the other end of the phone.

"We can keep trying". I said rubbing my forehead with a sigh.

"You're around babies all the time why can't you just get me one". She said before going silent.

"I-I can't do that". I said shaking my head.

"Don't you love me, Don't you want to raise a child and experience being a father". She asked and I nodded my head.

"Then get a baby for us are there any being born today". She asked as I looked through my papers.

"We have a few here now". I said and I can hear movement in the background.

"I'm coming up there to choose the perfect baby". She said before hanging up.

I know what we're doing is wrong but we've had five failed pregnancies and she deserves to be happy.

Standing up from my chair I make my way out of the office and to the nicu.

"Which baby is it". I ask looking at all the babies.

"This one right here sir she came in barely able to breath with multiple healing fracture wounds to the femur,septum, and fibula we hooked her up to an oxygen make but it isn't much help". A nurse said looking over at me from the child.

" Get her 5 mg of Albuterol every two hours and I'll come back and check on her". I said signing off on a paper.

"Sir your wife is here". Another nurse said causing me to turn around and see my wife Gayle.

"Let's go to the healthy babies". She asked looking around.

Taking her hand I lead her to the newborn room. She let's go of my hand and started looking at the babies and no one questioned it because she volunteers in the nursery a lot.

"Do you see one you like". I ask as she walked to each bed looking at them.

"Just let me stay and hold a few". She said and I nodded.

"I have to go there's a patient waiting for me". I said before walking out.

Knocking on the door I walk into the room.

"Hello I'm here to see how far along you're dilated". I said washing my hands and putting on gloves before sitting in front of her and lifting the cover.

Checking her she was already 10 cm dilated.

"Let's get started". I said putting my mask on.

•JAHREEM•

I held Marlowes hand the whole time as she pushed. When the baby was finally out this rope looking thing was around her neck and she wasn't crying and Marlowe started to panic causing me to panic.

"Why isn't she crying". She asked with tears in her eyes watching as the nurse passed her off to another and they took her out of the room.

"This happens and the babies end up just fine majority of the time". The doctor said as we nodded.

He washed his hands and left the room.

"She gone be okay". I said and she shook her head.

I lean down kissing Marlowe trying to sooth her as she continued to cry.

|Nursery|

Walking in I see my wife holding a baby with a huge smile on her face.

"I found the one". She said and I walked over seeing the baby I just delivered.

"Look put her down and go wait downstairs at the back doors". I said looking around and she nodded putting the baby down and walking away.

I run my hands down my face when someone taps my shoulder.

"Dr. Louis the baby brought in has passed away". One of the nurses said.

"Time of death". I ask looking through the paperwork on the clipboard she held.

"12:05 pm". She said and I nod signing off on it.

"I'll go and get her prepared to be moved". She said but I stopped her before she left.

"No, no I'll handle it". I said and she nodded.

Deeply sighing I get myself together and walk back to the room.

Standing outside of the door with my hand on the handle I say a quick prayer.

God forgive me...

PLEASE EXCUSE ANY MISTAKES #COMMENT#VOTE

Chapter 6

● DR.LOUIS•

Pushing the door open I walk in with a sad look on my face as they looked over at me.

"How is she". The young man asked with a look of concern holding the girls hand.

"I'm sorry we did all we can". I said before the young girl started to cry.

"Please man not my baby girl". He said shaking his head and his eyes started to tear up.

"Can we see her". The young girl asked looking over at me.

"Y-yes but only for a few minutes". I said walking out of the room.

Making my way to the Nicu I grab the deceased baby that was brought in that looked a little similar to theirs.

Wrapping it in a blanket I carried it to their room and open the door. Once their eyes laid on the baby in my hands they cried harder.

Walking over I place the baby in her arms and backed away.

|10 minutes later|

"Alright I have to take her". I said walking over and the young man kissed the little girls head before trying to hand her to the young women but she shook her head no.

Walking over I take the baby away and walk out. I see a nurse headed to where they handled the deceased.

"Would you mind taking her to get processed". I said stopping him and he nodded taking the baby from me.

Making my way to the nursery I look around to see if anybody was around before picking up the baby and making my way to the stairs.

After making it down the last few steps I push the door open and my wife looks over before making her way over to me taking the baby.

"Go home and I'll be there after my shift". I said and she nodded kissing me before making her way to the car.

Watching as she strapped the baby into the car seat she gets inside the car starting it up and pulling off.

Going back inside the building I go up the stairs to my floor and I continue my shift as if nothing happened.

"Dr.Louis we need you in room 310". A nurse said walking up to me and I follow behind her.

Hopefully this takes my mind off of what I had just done.

•MARLOWE•

Chapter 6

● DR.LOUIS•

Pushing the door open I walk in with a sad look on my face as they looked over at me.

"How is she". The young man asked with a look of concern holding the girls hand.

"I'm sorry we did all we can". I said before the young girl started to cry.

"Please man not my baby girl". He said shaking his head and his eyes started to tear up.

"Can we see her". The young girl asked looking over at me.

"Y-yes but only for a few minutes". I said walking out of the room.

Making my way to the Nicu I grab the deceased baby that was brought in that looked a little similar to theirs.

Wrapping it in a blanket I carried it to their room and open the door. Once their eyes laid on the baby in my hands they cried harder.

Walking over I place the baby in her arms and backed away.

|10 minutes later|

"Alright I have to take her". I said walking over and the young man kissed the little girls head before trying to hand her to the young women but she shook her head no.

Walking over I take the baby away and walk out. I see a nurse headed to where they handled the deceased.

"Would you mind taking her to get processed". I said stopping him and he nodded taking the baby from me.

Making my way to the nursery I look around to see if anybody was around before picking up the baby and making my way to the stairs.

After making it down the last few steps I push the door open and my wife looks over before making her way over to me taking the baby.

"Go home and I'll be there after my shift". I said and she nodded kissing me before making her way to the car.

Watching as she strapped the baby into the car seat she gets inside the car starting it up and pulling off.

Going back inside the building I go up the stairs to my floor and I continue my shift as if nothing happened.

"Dr.Louis we need you in room 310". A nurse said walking up to me and I follow behind her.

Hopefully this takes my mind off of what I had just done.

•MARLOWE•

I felt like with every breathe it was getting harder to breath I just don't understand what went wrong I did everything right.

"Calm down breath". Jahreem said rubbing my hand.

"I don't know what I did wrong I'm so sorry Jahreem". I said crying turning my head away from him.

"Baby it's not your fault okay maybe it wasn't our time". He said kissing my forehead and moving hair out of my face.

"She looked so peaceful". I said staring at the blank tv.

"I know and we can try again some day okay". He said but I shook my head.

"I don't want to". I said before looking over towards the door that opened.

"Hello I just came to let you know that you'll be released tomorrow after we keep an eye out for you tonight". She said but I didn't say anything.

"Thank you". Jahreem said and she nodded her head walking out of the room.

"She would have had a beautiful name". I said looking at the ceiling.

"And we can still name her what was the name you chose". He asked pulling his chair closer to the bed.

"Haisley Sky Mitchell". I said with a small smile on my face.

"It's beautiful just like her she would love that name". He said placing a kiss on my lips.

"Get some rest I'll be over there". He said pointing to the couch.

"Can you lay with me". I ask looking up at him.

"Yeah". He said nodding before getting in beside me and pulling me into him.

"I love you and I thank you for giving me a daughter". He said rubbing my arm causing me to smile.

"I love you too". I said closing my eyes with a sigh listening to his heartbeat.

He makes me feel safe...

PLEASE EXCUSE ANY MISTAKES #COMMENT#VOTE

Chapter 7

●JAHREEM•

I woke up early to go home and take a bath and also get Marlowe some clothes so that I can bring her home.

I'm back at the hospital signing her out while she gets dressed.

"We do have groups for mothers who loss their child in child birth maybe she would like to go and talk with other mothers who've experienced it". The nurse said as I handed the clipboard back to her.

"Where and what time does the groups get together". I ask and she starts writing on a piece of paper.

"There's a center downtown and they meet up at 2:00 every Tuesday and Thursday for about an hour and a half". She said and I nodded taking the paper she was holding out to me.

"Thank you". I said reading the address.

"No problem". She said before walking out.

Marlowe still wasn't out of the bathroom yet and she been in there for like 20 minutes. Walking over to the door I press my ear against it and I could hear the water running but I could also hear crying.

"Baby open the door". I said knocking on it.

Hearing it unlock I walk in and she's on the floor with her knees to her chest.

"It's okay baby". I said taking a seat by her on the floor.

"I don't want to go home without her". She said as I rubbed her back.

"I don't either but she's in a good place watching over us you think she would want to see you crying". I ask and she shook her head no.

"You're strong and you can overcome this now let's go". I said helping her up.

Walking out of the bathroom I grab the bags and follow out of the room behind her. Taking the elevator we make it to the first floor in no time and walk out of the building.

Tossing the bags in the back seat I go over and help her in the car before getting in myself. Starting it up I back out and pull off.

|Home|

Pulling into the parking lot I cut the car off and grab the bags before helping Marlowe out.

Walking into the apartment building we walk down the hall till we reach our door. Unlocking it we walk in and I drop the bags by the door.

"It's so quiet without her". She whispered and I tried to pull her into a hug but she walked away.

Following behind her we come to a stop in front of Haisley's shut room door that had fairies and butterflies on it. She reached out and touched the door before walking away to our room.

Taking her shoes off she gets in bed and throws the cover over her head. Taking my shoes off I get in beside her.

|4 hours later|

Waking up I feel the side of the bed and Marlowe wasn't there.

"Marlowe". I call out getting out the bed.

"Marlowe". I said looking in the bathroom.

Walking out of the room I start to make my way to the living room when I pass by Haisley's room and her door was opened.

Backing up I look inside and see Marlowe on the floor talking to herself rocking back and forth.

"I didn't kill her". She said to herself pulling at her hair.

"Yes you did you irresponsible bitch". She said to herself with a smirk on her face.

"I didn't...I didn't". She mumbled hitting herself.

"Hey hey hey stop". I said rushing over to her grabbing her arms.

"They're saying I killed her". She said as I stood her up.

"Come with me let's take a nap". I said closing the door and taking her to our room.

"She...I had her...where is she". She said looking around.

"Lay down with me". I said pulling her into my chest as I laid back.

"Where is she". She kept mumbling.

|2 hours later|

She finally fell asleep a few minutes ago after asking where is she for the last two hours.

Sliding from under her I make my way out of the room and close the door. Walking down the hall I stop in front of Haisley's room.

Holding the knob I take a deep breath before going in.

Walking over I run my hand along the crib rail before going over to the dresser by the rocking chair that held her ultrasound.

Picking it up I take a seat in the chair and just stare at the picture.

"I had so much planned for us babygirl it's like this shit ain't even real". I said talking to the picture and I saw a tear drop hit it.

"I was changing for you I was gone be the best father to you". I said sniffling as I ran my hand down my face.

I lay my head back and close my eyes holding the picture to my chest.

We would have been inseparable...

PLEASE EXCUSE ANY MISTAKES #COMMENT#VOTE

Chapter 8

A few few days later| •MARLOWE•

I've been in Haisley's room almost everyday all day I just can't bring myself to leave out of here. And the more I look at her crib I think about walking in here when she cries or coming in here in the morning when she wakes up.

"What you doing". Jahreem asked walking inside the room.

"Thinking about what I did wrong". I said tearing up as I sat in the rocking chair.

"Baby you didn't do anything wrong". He said kneeling down in front of me.

"I just look at this room and it makes me think about her". I said wiping my face.

She would have loved playing in here.

•JAHREEM•

"Look I'll pack everything up in the room and put it in storage". I said and she shook her head.

"No keep it the way it is she might come back". She said causing me to sigh.

"Baby she's gone she's not coming back". I said softly trying to touch her but she pushed me away.

"DON'T FUCKING SAY THAT DO YOU NOT CARE ABOUT HER AT ALL". She yelled causing me to look at her like she was crazy.

"OH COURSE I CARE ABOUT MY FUCKING DAUGHTER I BEEN TRYING TO HOLD SHIT TOGETHER FOR YOU". I yelled and I could feel veins popping out of my neck.

"You don't act like you care that she died". She said with a shrug.

"Let me get the fuck out of here before I say some shit". I said walking out of the room and grabbing the keys from the counter and walking out.

Going down the street to the grocery market I see some of my boys hanging out around there.

"Wassup dude how's the baby". One of the guys asked.

"Don't worry about it and come here let me talk to you". My bestfriend Rich said and we walk away from the group.

"What's going on I saw the look on your face when he asked". He said looking at me waiting for me to answer.

"She-she died man". I said tearing up and he pulled me into a hug.

"It's gone being okay man you got to stay strong for Marlowe". He said and I shook my head.

"That's what I been trying to do but it seems like she pushing me away". I said with a sigh looking at people that passed by.

"This just a hard time try not to take it to heart she needs you right now so go home". He said and I nod letting him know I was listening.

"I'll catch you later". I said dapping him up before walking off.

|15 minutes later|

Walking into the apartment I see Marlowe in the corner again talking to herself again holding a knife. Rushing over I take the knife from her.

I think it's time to call the institute she got out of for her own safety.

Pulling out my phone I dial the number and it rings a few times before somebody picked up.

"Cornerstone Psychiatric Institution". The person said as I looked at Marlowe.

"Wassup I have a released patient who isn't doing to good". I said and I could hear movement on the other end.

"Can I have the patients name please". She asked and I nodded.

"Marlowe Thompson". I said and she looked over at me before talking to herself again.

"And what is the problem". She asked typing on the computer.

"She uh talks to herself like hears voices that tell her to do things I don't know what it's called". I said scratching the back of my neck.

"I have her file up right now and I'm sending some people over to pick her up as we speak". She said and I nod as if she could see me.

"Cool thanks". I said before hanging up.

|25 minutes later|

I sat here watching Marlowe the whole time when a knock came on the door. Standing up I open the door and two dudes wearing all white stood there.

"She's over there". I said pointing at her as I moved to the side.

I watched as they went over and tried talking to her to see if she would go willingly but she wouldn't.

"We're going to have to pick her up is that alright". One of them asked me.

"Yeah don't hurt her though". I said and he nodded.

They picked her up and she started thrashing around swinging wildly.

"DON'T LET THEM TAKE ME". She screamed reaching out to me.

"Administer 30 mgs of Benzodiazepines lorazepam". One of them said to the other.

I watch as he pulled out a needle and stuck it in her arm and after that she went limp.

"Yo what did you just do". I ask with my face scrunched up.

"It's a sedative for aggressive patients she'll be fine". He said and I nodded.

They start walking out of the apartment and put her into an ambulance type of van.

Before they could close the door I stopped them.

"Let me say something to her real quick". I say and they nod letting me step in the van.

"I love you and I'm doing this for you". I said grabbing her hand kissing it.

"I-I love y-you too". She said slurring her words.

Stepping off the van they close the door and get in before driving off.

Dropping my head I shake it before walking back into the building and to our apartment.

I just want her to get the help she needs right now...

PLEASE EXCUSE ANY MISTAKES #COMMENT#VOTE

Chapter 9

---

5 months later| •MARLOWE•

I never thought I would be back in here so soon but I've been taking my medicine and getting better. Jahreem visits me literally everyday never misses a day.

"Knock knock". Someone said causing me to look up from Haisley's ultrasound picture.

"Hey". I said smiling standing up.

"Hey baby how you been". Jahreem said with a huge smile on his face.

"Good I miss you I'm ready to come home". I said with a pout on my face as he brung me into a hug.

"I know I miss you too". He said as we take a seat on my bed.

"I bought you some Hot Cheetos". He said pulling the bag out waving it in my face causing me to smile.

"What about my chips ahoy". I ask with my eyebrow raised.

"Come on now you know be better than that, BAM". He said whipping them out of the bag.

"Thank you". I said kissing him as he smiled.

And we sat there in silence.

"You know she would have been have been 5 months today". I said laying my head on his shoulder.

"I sometimes wonder what her smile would look like, what she smelled like, what she looks like". He said looking off to the side.

"I know you don't want to but do you want to visit her grave today". He said looking over at me.

I don't want to see her like that but maybe it'll help me come to terms with it.

"Yeah I'll go". I said lowly while nodding.

"Really". He asked in shock since he's been asking me for a while now.

"Yeah". I said with a half smile.

"Put your shoes and jacket on and let's go". He said and I nod standing up.

Grabbing my jacket I throw it on before putting on my shoes. Grabbing my hand he leads me to the front desk.

"I'd like to sign her out for 2 hours". He said to sally the front desk lady.

"Sign here". She said pointing to a clipboard on the desk.

He signed it and we walked out of the building. He opened the door for me and I got in.

Looking out of the window I see people walking the streets as he got in starting the car up. As he pulled off I cut the radio on.

|30 minutes later|

Getting out of the car I grab Jahreems hand because I don't know where her tombstone is.

We walked for a minute or two before we came in front of an angel tombstone and he stopped.

"This is her". He said looking down at it.

"I can't look". I said turning my head as tears began to form.

"Take a seat". He said pulling me down and I continued to look at the ground.

Looking up I see her name engraved.

"You have anything you want to say". He asked looking over at me and I shook my head.

"Not right now". I said and he nodded.

"Hey babygirl it's daddy again and I finally brought mommy with me". He said as I stared at the tombstone.

"You know when you were inside mommies tummy and I would play music for you and you would dance I just knew you would be a dancer I was going to take you to classes and dance with you". He said tearing up and I pulled him into me and he started crying into my chest.

|1 hour later|

We got up and started heading towards the car.

"You want some frozen yogurt". He asked as he opened my door.

"Yeah". I said nodding and he closed the door walking around the car getting in.

Leaning back I watch as building pass by as he drove.

Since the yogurt place wasn't far we made it there in five minutes. Getting out he throws his arm over my shoulder as we walk in.

We pick our cup and what flavor and toppings we wanted before going to the counter and paying. Walking over we take a seat at a table by the window.

"How's work been". I ask eating some of my yogurt.

"Good I got a 25 cent raise it's not much but it adds up". He said smiling cause me to smile.

The bell on the door run and I looked over seeing a lady pushing a stroller in. She walks past our table and I look at the baby and I see a heart shaped birthmark just like the one our daughter had.

"That's her that's our baby girl". I mumbled to myself staring at the baby in the stroller.

"What".He asked looking at me confused.

"That's our daughter". I said louder this time standing up and making my way over to the lady that just walked in.

"PUT ME DOWN THAT'S MY BABY I KNOW IT". I yell as he carries me outside putting me in the car and getting in himself.

"What is wrong with you". He asked looking over at me as he drove.

"That was our daughter". I said and he shook his head.

"That wasn't our daughter Marlowe you can't just go up saying peoples daughter is ours". He said and I didn't say anything the rest of the ride.

|25 minutes later|

We made it back to the institute and I got out walking inside the building.

As he signed me in I make my way to my room.

"Look". He started but I cut him off.

"I'm pretty tired I think you should go". I said taking off my jacket and shoes.

"Really Marlowe". He asked as I laid on the bed.

"Bye". I said turning facing the wall.

"I love you". He said as I stared at the wall.

"I love you too". I said and I could hear him walk out of the room closing the door.

Letting out a sigh I close my eyes.

That was my baby I just know it...

PLEASE EXCUSE ANY MISTAKES #COMMENT#VOTE

Chapter 10

● MARLOWE•

    Walking around the facility I looked around for Ike because he wasn't in the office like he usually was. When I got to the gaming area he was standing by the wall watching everybody.

Walking over he looks at me before a smile came on his face.

"Hey Marlowe how are you sweetheart". He said as he gave me a hug.

"I'm fine I was wondering if you could take me to the hospital". I said looking around the room.

"You killed her".I heard somebody say causing me to turn around quickly but no one was there.

"What's wrong". Ike said causing me to look back over at him.

"You didn't hear that". I ask looking at him with my eyebrows raised.

"Hear what". He asked with a confused look.

"You weren't ready to be a mother". The voice said again.

"That, you can't tell me you to don't hear that". I said and he shook his head.

"So the hospital why do you need to go". He asked pushing up from off the wall.

" I saw my baby a few days ago I just know it was her". I said and he sighed shaking his head.

"What". I ask with a frown on my face.

"You know I'm with you on anything but she's gone sweetheart". He said trying to touch my shoulder but I snatch away.

"Don't-don't say that she I-I saw her". I said staring at the ground in disbelief.

"She was there I saw her". I mumbled over and over to myself pulling my hair.

"Marlowe". He said reaching out to touch me and I swung at him.

"I SAW HER I SAW HER". I yelled hitting him and I could hear footsteps before I felt people picking me up.

Feeling a pinching sensation in my upper arm I stop moving and my eyes start to feel heavy. Looking over I see Ike looking at me with sympathy.

"I'm sorry". I said slowly reaching my hand out to him.

"It's okay sweetheart just get some rest". He said rubbing my hand and I nod slowly as they carry me away.

•JAHREEM•

Putting on my work boots I was in deep thought about Marlowe thinking our daughter was alive I mean the shit couldn't be true I held her and she didn't move nor was she breathing.

"What's on your mind young man". A voice said causing me to look up.

"A lot of shit but I need to get out there to get started". I said standing up.

Walking out of the locker room I grabbed keys off the wall since I was driving forklifts today.

Getting on the forklift I cut it on and back out.

"You got a pick up on the east side of the warehouse". One of my supervisors said and I nodded driving off.

|10 hours later|

Putting my shoes in the locker I close it and walk out of the locker room. Scanning my id I walk out the doors and to my car starting it up I pull off.

It took me about 20 to 25 minutes to make it home and when I pulled into the parking lot I look around seeing nobody.

Getting out the car I lock the doors and walk inside the building. Unlocking the front door I walk in closing and locking the door. Tossing my keys on the table before walking to the back.

I pass by Haisley's door that was open and look inside. I could see her holding onto the side of the crib bouncing up and down smiling once she saw me.

Shaking my head I close the door and make my way to our room. Taking a seat on the bed I put my head in my hands as my knee bounced up and down.

I don't know what came over me but I start knocking shit over and punching the walls.

Putting a hole in the door I slide down it.

"Fuck man". I mumble to myself as my head fell.

I don't know how long I can keep acting like I'm okay...

Chapter 11

● MARLOWE•

Hearing a knock on my door I look over from my painting at the door and see Jahreem.

"What are you doing here". I ask with a confused look.

"I came to get you out baby". He said causing me to smile as he walked over and bring me into a hug.

"But I have a few more months left". I said and he shook his head.

"No I'm taking you out today". He said as he held me.

"I can't I'm still not better I still believe she's alive". I said shaking my head.

"And I believe you". He said causing me to look at him.

"You do". I ask and he nods his head yes.

"If you believe that baby was our little girl I believe you". He said causing me to smile.

Bringing his head down I peck his lips over and over as he laughed.

"Alright pack your stuff I'm about to sign you out". He said pulling out of the hug.

"Okay". I said walking over to the closet as he walked out.

•JAHREEM•

Walking to the front desk they were standing around talking.

"Aye excuse me I would like to sign Marlowe Thompson out". I said and they all looked over at me.

"No problem let me just get her papers ready". The lady said and I nodded looking around and I could feel somebody looking at me.

"Is there a problem". I ask tilting my head to the side.

"She's not ready to leave she still thinks her dead baby is alive and you think it's a good idea to take you out". He said as I scrunched my face up.

"I'm sorry who are you". I ask with my eyebrows scrunched up.

"I'm Cody". He said walking up to the other side of the desk.

"Oh okay I thought you were her dad but what I'm doing has nothing to do with you and if I say she's good then she good". I said and he shook his head.

"But she's not she needs to be here where she can get better". He said causing me to laugh non-humorously.

"Don't tell me what my girl needs I wouldn't put her in a situation I know she can't handle so mind your business before I come across this desk". I say staring at him as I spoke.

"I'm ready". I heard from behind me causing me to turn around with a smile on my face.

"Hey baby I just got to sign your papers". I said and she nodded going to take a seat.

"Sorry for the long wait here her papers you just have to sign where the x's are". The girl said handing me a pin and I took it signing the papers.

Once I was done I gave her everything back.

"Let's go". I said looking over at Marlowe and she stood up grabbing my hand.

We walk out and I put her stuff up as she got in the car.

"Where are we starting first". She asked looking over at me.

"The hospital". I said starting the car up and pulling off.

|30 minutes later|

Parking the car we get out and walk inside. Going up to the front desk we wait until the man gets off the phone before talking.

"Excuse me can we speak to doctor Louis". Marlowe said leaning against the counter.

"He's in the delivery room at the moment he's almost done why don't you take a seat". He said and we nodded going to sit down.

"Do you really believe me or are you just doing this because I'm crazy". Marlowe asked once we sat down.

"Yo you not crazy, if you say that was our daughter then that's our daughter". I said and she smiled laying her head on my shoulder.

|15 minutes later|

Looking up from my phone I see doctor Louis at the counter talking to the man before they both looked our way and he walked over.

"How may I help you". He said as I shook Marlowe awake.

"We want to see the papers that show how our daughter died". Marlowe said and he shook his head.

"She didn't have any oxygen going to her brain". He said with a sad look.

"So show us the paper that tells us that I want to see papers about the test that were ran on her". I said and he shook his head.

"Come to my office so we can discuss this". He said and I shook my head.

"Look are you going to give us the papers or not". I ask slightly raising my voice.

"Look I've told you already she didn't have oxygen getting to her brain". He said and I nodded grabbing Marlowe's hand walking out.

"So that's it we're just giving up". She asked looking over at me as we got in the car.

"Nah I got a plan". I said starting it up and pulling off.

We getting them papers one way or another...

PLEASE EXCUSE ANY MISTAKES #COMMENT#VOTE

Chapter 12

Hospital| •MARLOWE•

Parking the car he looks over at me as I do the same.

"I been coming to this hospital to see where his office was and I found it so while I distract them I want you to go in there and look for Haisleys file". He said handing me a paper and I nodded.

"What about cameras". I ask looking from the hospital to him.

"That's why I made you go back in the house as get that mask and jacket". He said cutting the car off.

"Let me walk in first and then you come in and stand off to the side". He aid getting out of the car before making his way to my side.

I was so tired I wasn't really comprehending what was going on.

"Hey look at me". He said grabbing my face.

"You can do this we ain't no punks". He said causing us to laugh.

"We can do this". I said over and over nodding my head.

"That's right gimme a kiss". He said poking his lips out.

"I love you baby". He said staring into my eyes.

"I love you too". I said getting out of the truck.

He starts to walk in and a minute or two later I walk in standing off the the side.

"I need to see doctor Louis now". Jahreem said but the receptionist shook her head.

"I'm sorry I can't do that". She said as a few people looked on.

"HE DROPPED MY CHILD AND YOU CAN'T GET HIM". He yelled and all the women gasped looked over before standing up getting ready to leave.

"Wait wait wait this is a misunderstanding right sir". She said looking over at Jahreem.

"You getting doctor Louis". He asked and she nodded her head.

"Then yeah I'm just fucking with y'all". He said causing me to laugh.

I pull out the paper and see it's a way to get to the office. Since my mask was already on I make my way to the stairs looking around before going up them.

Once I made it to the 6th floor I look around and no one was up there and it was quiet. Walking into his office I look at the filing cabinet and start to go through it.

Going through the alphabet I stop at H and look for Haisleys name. Finding it I pull it out and before I could look at it I hear voices outside the door.

Quickly getting underneath the desk I open the file and take pictures of all the pages.

Snapping a picture of the last page the door opens.

"How's the baby doing I miss her already".He said and my eyebrows went up as he sat down in the chair in front of me.

He never told us he had a child nor was it stated on the internet. The office phone begin to ring and he answered it.

"Okay I'll be right down". He said before hanging up.

"Honey I have to go some man is causing a disturbance I'll call you later". He said before hanging up and I see him standing up before hearing the door open and close.

Quickly getting from under the desk I put the file back and open the door looking both ways before going back down the staircase.

"I'm not leaving this damn hospital until you tell these people you drop babies". Jahreem said mugging Dr. Louis as people looked to see what was going on.

"Sir I assure you I do not drop babies". Dr. Louis said and Jahreem was about to say something else before he saw me.

"Alright bye". He said as I made my way out of the hospital.

Getting in the car I wait for him and he finally gets in looking over at me.

"You got it". He asked and I waved my phone and he smiled before starting the car up and pulling off.

"Now what do we do". I ask looking over at him as he drove.

"We gone pull it up on the laptop at home". He said and I nodded sitting back.

|HOME|

Cutting the car off we got out and made our way inside. Jahreem went to get the laptop so that we could pull it up.

"Give it here". He said holding his hand out and I gave him my phone.

I sat there as he typed and stuff before the pictures popped up. We started reading through them silently.

"It doesn't say anywhere in there that she died". He said cause me to look at him.

"So that means she's alive right". I ask looking over at him.

"Baby its a huge possibility I got to be at work in a few but when I get off tomorrow morning we going straight to the police station". He said and I nodded my head.

"Go get some sleep". He said kissing my forehead as he stood up.

Doing the same I follow him to our room looking at Haisleys in the way.

As he got dressed I laid in bed watching him.

"Alright I'm about to go show me some love". He said poking his lips out.

Kissing him a huge smile graced his face as he stared at me.

"I love you". He said still staring at me.

"I love you too". I said getting comfortable.

"I'll see you in the morning". He said before walking out.

Picking up the remote I flip through channels before deciding on the discovery channel.

If what he said was true then I could possibly be right...

PLEASE EXCUSE ANY MISTAKES #COMMENT#VOTE

Chapter 13

•JAHREEM•

Getting out of the car I hit the lock button before walking into the building.

Walking trough the front door I didn't hear anything letting me know that Marlowe was still asleep.

Making my way to the back I open the room door and see her knocked out causing me to laugh. Since it was only 3 in the morning I decided to take a quick shower and get in bed.

Cutting on the shower water I go grab some clothes before taking mines off and stepping in.

|15 minutes later|

Stepping out of the shower I grab a big towel and wrap it around my waist before picking up my dirty clothes and throwing them in the hamper.

Drying off I slip my shorts on and walk out of the bathroom.

Pulling the covers back I get in bed and pull Marlowe towards me and she lays her head on my chest.

|8:15am|

Feeling something like me I open my eyes and see Marlowe fully dressed.

"Get up we have to go". She said and I nodded sitting up.

Throwing the cover off of me I stand up and stretch before walking into the closet to find something to wear.

After getting dressed I walk to the living room and Marlowe was sitting on the couch watching tv.

"You ready to go". I ask and she nods standing up.

Walking to the car we get in and I start it up and pull off.

•MARLOWE•|Police station|

We finally made it to the station and I'm kind of nervous.

"You ready to go in here". He asked looking over at me.

"Yeah". I said nodding my head and we get out walking inside.

"Excuse me can we talk to an office or somebody". Jahreem asked and they just kept walking past him.

"EXCUSE ME CAN I SPEAK WITH SOMEBODY". He yelled causing everybody to look over and somebody walked up.

"Can I help you". An office said walking up to us.

"As a matter a fact you can my girlfriend gave birth not to long ago but they told us the baby died but the files have no information regarding the death". He said and the officer nodded.

"Maybe the doctor forgot to put the information in". He said causing me to scrunch up my face.

"So can you look into it because we think she's still alive". I said and he started laughing.

"Ma'am I'm sure there was a mix up there's nothing we can do sorry". He said walking away and I walked up to him turning him around.

"There's nothing you can do are you shitting me right now y'all are all sitting on your asses doing nothing and you can't go to the hospital and at least check". I ask raising my voice as everyone looked over.

"Ma'am if you put your hands on me again I'm going to have to arrest you". He said and I looked over at Jahreem and he shook his head.

I reached my hand out to touch him again when I was pulled away and out of the building.

"Why did you do that". I ask as we got in the car.

"Cause your ass was about to be arrested". He said starting the car up and pulling off.

"So what do we do now they won't help us". I said with a sigh.

"Hire a private investigator to follow Dr. Louis". He said looking over at me.

"You have an answer for everything but that's not a bad idea and I saw a picture on his desk of him and his wife and she looked familiar". I said racking my brain trying to think.

Yesterday when I was getting from under the desk I saw a picture of them sitting on his desk but I was in such a rush I didn't get a good look.

"I'm still mad that they couldn't do anything". He said gripping the steering wheel.

"That's complete bullshit they could help they just didn't want to". I said rolling my eyes as I sat back into the seat.

"Don't worry baby he gone have to answer for this". He said rubbing my thigh and I nodded my head.

It's okay though because we were going to get to the bottom of this one way or another...

PLEASE EXCUSE ANY MISTAKES #COMMENT#VOTE

Chapter 14

A few days later|

•MARLOWE•

We were finally able to schedule a meeting with a private investigator which took a couple of days because they had so many people coming in.

Right now we're sitting outside his office waiting to be called in.

"How you feeling". Jahreem asked looking over at me.

"Kind of nervous I don't know what to expect like what if he's not able to help us". I said running my hands up and down my pants.

"I did my research and he seemed like the most qualified so I have no doubt he'll be able to help us". He said grabbing my hand and the office door swung open and there stood a man.

"Hello I'm PI Stanley". He said walking over and shaking our hand.

"Nice to meet you my name is Marlowe and this is Jahreem". I said pointing to Jahreem beside me.

"Come into my office so we can talk privately". He said gesturing for us to walk in first.

Taking a seat in front of the desk he walks around and takes a seat as well.

"So tell me what can I do for you". He asked looking between me and Jahreem.

"So my girlfriend gave birth a few months back and the baby came out not breathing so they took her away and later on told us she died". Jahreem said and the man nodded.

"So you want me to figure out how she died". He asked and we shook our head no.

"We believe she is still alive just look at the paperwork on her and she has this birthmark that I saw on her when she was born and one day when we were having ice cream a lady walked in with a baby that had the same birthmark in the exact same place". I said pulling out the pages we printed of the pictures I took handing them to him.

He looked over them while we sat in silence.

"So what exactly do you want me to do". He asked looking up.

"We want you to follow the doctor and also see if you can find our Baby-girl". I said as he stared at me.

"This might be a long process and I charge 3 thousand dollars". He said and my heart sank to my stomach.

"We don't have that kind of money". I said shaking my head.

"Can we do payment installments I get paid every week". Jahreem said and he shook his head.

"I'm sorry I can't do that". He said and I dropped my head trying not to cry.

"Thank you for your time". I said standing up and we start walking to the door.

"I see how much this means to you guys so I'm willing to do the installments". He said causing me to smile.

"Thank you so much". I said walking over and hugging him.

" I appreciate it man". Jahreem said shaking hands with him.

"I usually don't do this but you guys will only have to pay 1500". He said and I started crying because we literally have no money and for him to lower his price for us was so nice.

"Thank you man really". Jahreem said and he nodded his head.

"I'll be starting today and give you updates every couple of days". He said opening his office door.

"Alright thanks". I said as we walked out and out of the building.

"I can't believe he's actually going to help us". I said as we got into the car.

"And for him to bring his price down that was crazy". Jahreem said starting the car up.

"Do you have to go to work today". I ask looking over at him.

"Nah I'm off what you trying to do". He asked looking from the road to me.

"Can we go by the institute". I ask and he nodded.

|Institute|

Getting out I walk inside and sign the paper to visit Brent.

We walk back to his room and he was just sitting on the bed reading a book.

"Brent". I called out and he looked over at me and stood up walking over giving me a hug.

"How have you been". He asked as he gave Jahreem a handshake.

"I've been okay how have you been". I ask taking a seat on his bed.

"I've been good". He said taking a seat beside me.

"Where you going all dressed up". Jahreem asked causing him to smile and look down at his clothes.

"Pamela is coming to visit me today". He said and I gave him a small smile.

"You sure she doesn't have to work today". I ask and he looks as if he was thinking.

"No she's off". He said and I nodded my head.

"Did you watch the game last night". Jahreem asked and Brents face lit up.

As they started talking about the game I sat there and looked between the two.

I have to come up and visit him more often...

PLEASE EXCUSE ANY MISTAKES #COMMENT#VOTE

Chapter 15

● MARLOWE•

Today we are meeting up with our PI guy because he says he has some things to show us. Jahreem is getting dressed since he just got home from work and I can tell he's super tired but since it's pertaining to Haisley he doesn't care.

"Hey baby I'm ready to go". He said walking from the back.

Standing up from the couch I follow him out and get in the car while he locks the door. Buckling my seatbelt he gets in starting it up and pulling off.

" You think he got some good news". He asked looking over at me.

"I hope so because I find myself questioning myself about it like is she really alive or am I just making this up to cope with the death of her, maybe I am crazy".I said and he reached over grabbing my hand.

"Aye don't say that shit again you're not crazy". He said causing me to laugh sarcastically.

"I'm not crazy but I have episodes where I talk to myself and hear voices in my head". I said and he shook his head.

"I'm not about to go there with you". He said releasing his hand.

Not saying anything else the rest of the ride was silent.

|CAFÉ|

Getting out I wait for Jahreem and he walks over grabbing my hand leading us inside.

I look around and spot the PI sitting in the back of the Café. Tapping Jahreem arm he looks down at me and I point to the PI.

Making our way over he looks up before standing up to greet us.

"Hello". He said shaking our hand.

"Hello". I said as we all took a seat and I couldn't help but look at the manila folder on the table.

"So I've been following that doctor like you asked me to and I've also done some research". He said picking up the folder and opening it pulling out papers.

"So his record is clean no DUIs, no arrests, no traffic stops, tickets nothing but I followed him home and sat outside his house and he was greeted by a lady with a child". He said and we nodded as we listened.

"So what does that have to do with figuring out what happened to our daughter". Jahreem asked and I wanted to know to.

"Well as I was doing research it didn't come up that he had any children so it was odd for that little girl to be there and she's there everyday all day". He said sliding the paper over to us.

"Also I spoke to the nurses that took the baby out of the room and they said they got her to breath and she was indeed breathing on her own so they placed her in the nursery". He said and I nod listening to him.

As we read over them I could hear him doing something else.

"I also took some pictures of the little girl it's not very good ones it's a side shot and they're kind of blurry they don't really bring her out of the house". He said sliding the pictures across the table to us.

Looking down at the picture I pick it up staring at her and then I looked over at the lady that was holding her.

"Tha-that's her that's the lady from the ice cream shop".I said pointing at her on the picture looking over at Jahreem.

He took the picture looking closely at the lady.

"Who is she". He asked because when we looked up Dr.Louis it said he had a wife but there was never any pictures of her.

"That's his wife". He said and I began to piece things together.

"So you're telling me that he and his wife don't have any kids yet here she is holding a little girl that has the same birthmark as my daughter in the same place". I ask and he sighs looking down at the table.

"They-they kidnapped my baby because how does a baby just disappear". I say to myself and I start to hear voices in my head causing me to grab my hair.

•JAHREEM•

I look over and see Marlowe spaces out before she started pulling at her hair.

"Um can you send that to us we need to leave". I said standing up.

"Yeah sure no problem". He said standing up from the table.

Grabbing Marlowe I pick her up and carry her outside to the car.

"He took her, they took her, she's alive". She mumbled to herself rocking back and forth.

"It's okay baby we're going to get her back okay". I said rubbing her thigh.

"They took her". She said hitting herself in the head and I reached over grabbing her wrist in my hand.

I held her like that all the way to the apartment and once we got there I got out and went to her side getting her out.

Walking inside the apartment I unlock our door and walk in locking it behind me. Taking a seat on the couch I held Marlowe in my lap as she continued to try and hit herself but I held her arms kissing the side of her head.

I should have known information like that would trigger her...

PLEASE EXCUSE ANY MISTAKES #COMMENT#VOTE

Chapter 16

• MARLOWE•

Right now we are sitting in the courthouse with our lawyer trying to see if there is anything we could do to get a DNA test done on the little girl.

"Your honor we are here today to request that the police be sent to Dr. Louis's home immediately and the child be taken into custody until we get the test done and the results back". Our lawyer Grant said and I didn't even know they could do that so I was shocked but I didn't protest.

"And what information do you have that leads me to believe that this child could possibly be theirs, what you just want me to send officers to a well respected Drs home and arrest him". The judge said and I tilted my head to the side.

"That's exactly what he's saying". I said mugging him and Jahreem squeezes my hand softly causing me to look over at him and he shook his head no.

"Speak out of term again and I will dismiss the whole case". He said and I opened my mouth to say something else but then I thought about Haisley so I just sat back.

"So are you going to grant us that". Grant asked and the judge looked at him.

"I'll grant the DNA test but the child will stay with its parents and the test will be scheduled for tomorrow ". He said before getting his papers and standing up walking away.

"Fucking dickhead". I said as I stood up causing Grant and Jahreem to laugh.

"I'm going to keep trying to get him to agree with getting the child taken until we figure out this whole ordeal". Grant said picking up all the papers and putting them in his briefcase.

"Okay thank you and please update us if anything changes". I said shaking his hand and he nods.

Looking over at Jahreem I noticed that he hasn't said a word now that I think about it he hasn't really said much since we had the meeting with our PI.

"You ready to go". He asked and I nod following behind him.

Getting in the car I start it up and pull off.

"Why you been so quiet". I ask looking over at him then back at the road.

"I can't decide if I want to kill him and go to jail for life or let the police handle it and be with my daughter for the rest of her life". He said staring at the road.

"I think option two sounds a lot better". I said nodding.

"Yeah but the devil is dancing on option one and he looking real tempting". He said with a straight face.

"At least we get to do the test as soon as possible". I said trying to lighten the mood.

"She not gone want to be with us cause she don't know us". He said with a sigh dropping his head.

"I don't know how true this is but kids have connections with their parents". I said grabbing his hand with my free hand.

"I haven't really had time to process all this information and shit just hitting me left and right like if she is ours and we do get her I expect her to automatically come to me but I know that shit not gone happen". He said shaking his head.

"I mean you never know it could". I said parking the car and getting out.

Walking into the apartment building I unlock the door and walk in first.

"How about I make your favorite". I ask with a smile causing him to smile a little.

"I would really appreciate it baby". He said walking to the living room.

Going into the kitchen I get all the things I need to make his food and get started.

|2 hours later|

Picking up the plates I carry them to the living room and hand him his before sitting mines on the table and going to get us something to drink.

Taking a seat beside him we start eating while watching tv.

After we got done I took the plates to the kitchen placing them in the dishwasher before walking back to the living room.

When I got back Jahreem wasn't in there.

"BABY". I call out walking to the back.

"I'm in here". He said as I passed Haisley's room.

"When did you get that". I ask as he sat in the rocking chair holding a teddy bear.

"I bought it the other day you know if she's ours then she can play with it". He said looking down at it.

Walking over I take a seat by his legs and lay my head on his lap.

"She's going to love it". I said closing my eyes as he started running his fingers through my hair.

"I hope so". He mumbled but I still heard him.

She'll love him...

PLEASE EXCUSE ANY MISTAKES #COMMENT#VOTE

Chapter 17

Next Day|

•JAHREEM•

Today is the day we get the test done and I'm not gone lie I'm nervous as hell cause I don't know what to expect like if she's ours do we get to take her or do they take her.

"Baby you don't hear me calling you". Marlowe asked causing me to look over at her.

"Nah what did you need". I ask walking over to her.

"What time did they say we had to be there". She asked looking up at me.

"At 1:30 it's 12:30 right now but since we requested to go to the other hospital we need to leave now to make it in time". I said kissing her forehead.

"Alright let me go get my bag". She said and I nodded picking up this babydoll I bought Haisley.

"That's for Haisley". She asked as we walked out of the door.

"Yeah I thought maybe she'd like it". I said as we got in the car.

"It's cute". She said looking at it as I started the car up and pulled off.

|30 minutes later|

Pulling into the parking lot I cut the car off and get out walking around opening Marlowe's door. Grabbing my hand we both walk inside.

I look around and see our lawyer but not just our lawyer I see Dr. Luis and his wife who was holding a little girl and a man in a suit so I'm assuming he's their lawyer.

Before I even know what was happening Marlowe was running towards them about to hit Dr. Luis before I grabbed her up.

"You're fucking sick and both of you should be ashamed of yourselves". She said breathing heavily.

"Calm down". I said kissing the side of her forehead.

"I would appreciate if you didn't act that way in front of our daughter". The lady said causing me to mugging her.

"That's my daughter y'all are kidnappers come on now". Marlowe said with her face scrunched up.

I couldn't stop staring at the little girl I mean she was beautiful.

"Since you all are here early we can go ahead and get the test started so everyone follow me". The Dr said and we all followed behind him.

Walking into the room there weren't many chairs so I sat down and then pulled Marlowe onto my lap.

"So I'm going to start with you guys first now I'm going to swab your mouth and then you're going to hold it in your cheek for one minute". He said walking over to me and Marlowe with this long q-tip.

He did me first and while the q-tip was sitting on the side of my cheek he did Marlowe.

"Alright I'm going to take this".He sad taking it out of my mouth and putting it in a tube writing my name on it.

|15 minutes later|

After everybody got done getting tested he had someone come in and take the test to the lab.

"So usually it would take two weeks to get this information back because we have so many but since this is an expedited process it'll be done in a week". He said and as he was talking I was staring at Dr. Louis and his wife and he looked nervous but not his wife.

"Alright thank you". Our lawyer said and we stood up walking out.

As we made our way in the waiting room there were two cops and a lady with a badge and file in her hand between them.

"Greta glad you came on such short notice". Our lawyer said walking over and shaking the lady's hand.

"It's no problem just glad I can help so where is she". She asked and just as she asked that the dr and his wife walked in.

"What is going on here". Their lawyer asked walking up.

"By order of the court Kennedy has to go to the orphanage until the results come back". Our lawyer said.

"Were's the court order". He asked and our lawyer took it out of his jacket pocket handing it to him.

He read over it as everybody watched him.

"I'm sorry Dr. Louis she has to go with this lady". He said looking back at them.

"No my baby isn't going with them". The lady said holding onto the little girl tightly and when I looked at her she was already staring at me.

"Ma'am hand the baby over or we are going to have to use force and that might cause harm to the child". One of the officers said as they walked over to her.

She sighed before letting the little girl go but the girl started crying and screaming reaching for her.

I walk over handing the little girl the doll and she looked at me taking it but she still cried.

"Alright we will see you guys in a week". The social worker said before leaving.

Shaking my head I grab Marlowe's hand and walk out to the car.

Helping her in I get in myself and start the car up pulling off.

"She's ours I can feel it". Marlowe said causing me to look over at her.

"I know". I said and the rest of the ride was silent.

I'm ready for the results to come back...

PLEASE EXCUSE ANY MISTAKES #COMMENT#VOTE

Chapter 18

A week later| •MARLOWE•

I was so nervous right now because I'm just a hour we were going to find out if that little girl is ours or not.

"You okay". Jahreem asked brushing his teeth as he walked out of the bathroom.

"Yeah just nervous because I don't know the outcome". I said buttoning up my shirt as I sat on the bed.

"The way that little girl looked at me you can't tell me that's not my daughter". He said with a smile on his face.

"I'm surprised she actually took the bear from you that day". I said standing up grabbing my dress pants.

"Shit me too but I'm glad she did cause it had my voice recorded in it". He said wiping his face with a face towel.

"That's so sweet". I said with a smile on my face.

"Shit baby we need to hurry up". He said looking at the clock.

I look over and see we have thirty minutes to get to the courthouse.

|30 minutes later|

Pulling up outside we get out and he grabs my hand as we walk in. Looking over I see Dr Louis and his wife and the lady from the hospital with the little girl.

"Let's get started who has the results". The judge asked looking between the two lawyers.

"That would be me your honor". Our lawyer said handing the envelope to the office that walked over.

He handed them to the judge and he opened the envelope reading over it.

"It looks like that little girl does indeed belong to the Mitchell's". The judge said and I passed out.

•JAHREEM•

I feel something lean on me causing me to look down and see Marlowe passed out. Our lawyer handed me a paper and I started fanning her and after a good minute or so she woke up.

"She's ours that's Haisley". She asked looking at me and I nodded my head with a smile.

"Mr and Mrs Louis are set to spend 45 to life with no bail or possibility of parole and your license is also revoked". The judge said slamming the gavel.

Greta the social worker walked over and tried to hand Haisley to Marlowe but she started crying reaching for Mrs. Louis. She then tried giving her to me and she came without a problem laying her head into my neck.

"Thanks for helping us man". I said shaking hands with our lawyer.

"It's no problem really I'm just glad you guys caught on to this now and not when she was older". He said and I nodded.

"You ready to go". I ask looking over at Marlowe and she nodded grabbing my hand.

Walking out we get to the car and I go to strap Haisley in but she starts to cry.

"I'm gone sit back here with her". I said handing Marlowe the keys and getting in.

Leaning back Marlowe starts the car and pulls off.

|30 minutes later|

Walking into the house I had to use the bathroom so I handed Haisley to Marlowe and she started crying but I really had to piss so I went ahead and went.

Washing my hands I walk out and Haisley was still crying.

"Can you take her I just need a minute". Marlowe said handing her to me and walking away.

Looking down she was sniffling already looking up at me.

"What's wrong mama's". I ask walking to her room and taking a seat in the rocking chair.

Leaning back she lays her head on my chest and after a while I look down and she was sleep. Standing up I place her in her crib before walking out cracking the door.

Going to our room I walk in and Marlowe was crying.

"Baby what's wrong". I ask wrapping my arm around her.

"She hates me". She said and I shook my head.

"Baby she doesn't hate you she's just not used to you yet she's used to that other lady". I said kissing the side of her forehead.

"Then how come she goes to you so easily". She asked and I shrugged my shoulders.

"I can't really tell you that but what I can tell you is that when she gets used to you she gone want you all the time". I said causing her to smile.

"Let's take a nap while she sleep and then we can go do something when she wakes up". I said laying down and she did the same laying her head on my chest.

Looking up at the ceiling I start to wonder.

Why is she so willing to come to me...

The End

| 1 year later| •MARLOWE•

Putting the dishes away I walk over and place the bowel on Haisley's high chair before walking to the living room to go get her.

"Mama". She said reaching up for me causing me to smile as I picked her up.

It took a while for her to get used to me and start calling me that.

"What she eating". Jahreem said walking in stretching.

"Some applesauce". I said sitting her in the high chair.

"You know they got that new park opened up I was thinking we could take her". Jahreem said taking some of her applesauce.

"You trying to go when she gets done eating". I ask looking over at him.

"Yeah I'm about to go get changed". He said walking away.

"We going to the park mamas". I said watching her eat applesauce with her hands.

DISAPPEARANCE

|1 hour later|

After Haisley finished eating and Jahreem took his shower we go in the car to go to the park.

"You think it's going to be a lot of people there". He asked looking over at me as he drove.

"It might seeing as though the other parks got closed down". I said looking In the back to make sure that the baby was good.

"True but you know what I noticed". Jahreem asked grabbing my hand.

"What". I ask rubbing his hand.

"You haven't had no mental breakdowns". He said looking at me then back to the road.

"That's because I've been taking medication". I said staring at him.

"When you start back taking that". He asked with his face scrunched up.

"After we found out Haisley was ours and why you make that face". I asked with my eyebrow raised.

"Nah baby it's not like that I was just confused cause I didn't know you started taking it again but that's good for you". He said bringing my hand up kissing it causing me to smile.

Looking outside the window I see that we were at the park.

"We here daddy's baby". Jahreem said parking the car and getting out to get Haisley.

•JAHREEM•

Closing the door I carry Haisley as we walk up to the gate and pay.

"What you think she should ride first". I ask looking down at Marlowe.

"How about that Caterpillar ride over there". She said pointing at it and it was going at a good safe speed.

Nodding we walk over and get in line. Watching as the people go by they were waving I look down at Haisley and see her smiling and waving.

"Say this ride better not go no faster than this with my daughter on here". I said to the boy running the ride as we got on.

"Yes sir". He said checking out seat belts.

"You play to much". Marlowe said laughing as I just looked at her.

"I ain't playing this bitch better go five miles per hour or less". I said causing her to laugh harder.

"Please keep your hands and feet inside the ride at all times". The worker said before the ride started.

We started going around and Marlowe was having the time of her life.

"Weeee". She said grabbing Haisley's hands making faces causing her to laugh.

"She likes it". Marlowe said looking up at me.

"She laughing cause of them ugly ass faces you making". I said laughing as she straight faced me.

"Fuck you". She said playfully rolling her eyes.

After a few more minutes the ride was over and we got off.

"Where to next". Marlowe asked looking around.

"Y'all can go get on another ride but I'm about to go get a funnel cake with ice cream". I said and she shook her head.

"We going too let's go". She said walking off to the food truck with Haisley on her hip.

We ordered our stuff and went to go take a seat at the table as we waited.

"Jahreem". I heard somebody say and I got up walking up to the window grabbing our food.

"This looks so good". Marlowe said as I sat it on the table talk big a seat.

She grabbed a fork and reached out trying to get a piece but I pushed her hand back.

"What are you doing baby". She asked with a confused look on her face.

"This my babygirl first time with us trying a funnel cake and I want to see her reaction". I said pulling my phone out to record her.

Watching Marlowe get a little piece she put it up to Haisley's mouth and let her suck on it and she went crazy reaching for it causing us to laugh.

"I guess she like it". I said putting my phone away.

We started to eat and just enjoy each others company. Once we were done we rode a few more rides before Haisley knocked out at we left.

|1 hour later|

Pulling inside of the driveway I cut the car off and we get out walking inside. Locking the door I make my way to the back and see Haisley laying in the middle of the bed sleep and I could hear water running in the bathroom.

"You gone join me or what". Marlowe asked peeking her head outside the door.

Taking my clothes off I walk into the bathroom and step inside behind her. We washed up and got out going to lay in the bed on each side of Haisley.

"I love you". Marlowe said looking at me.

"I love you too". I said and she closed her eyes snuggling up to Haisley.

"I love you too babygirl". I said leaning down kissing her forehead.

I watched them sleep for a few minutes before I got tired.

It felt good to have a family and to think I wouldn't have had the chance because of Haisley's Disappearance.

www.ingramcontent.com/pod-product-compliance
Ingram Content Group UK Ltd.
Pitfield, Milton Keynes, MK11 3LW, UK
UKHW020243120225
454951UK00010B/430